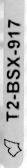

THE GREAT BEAR

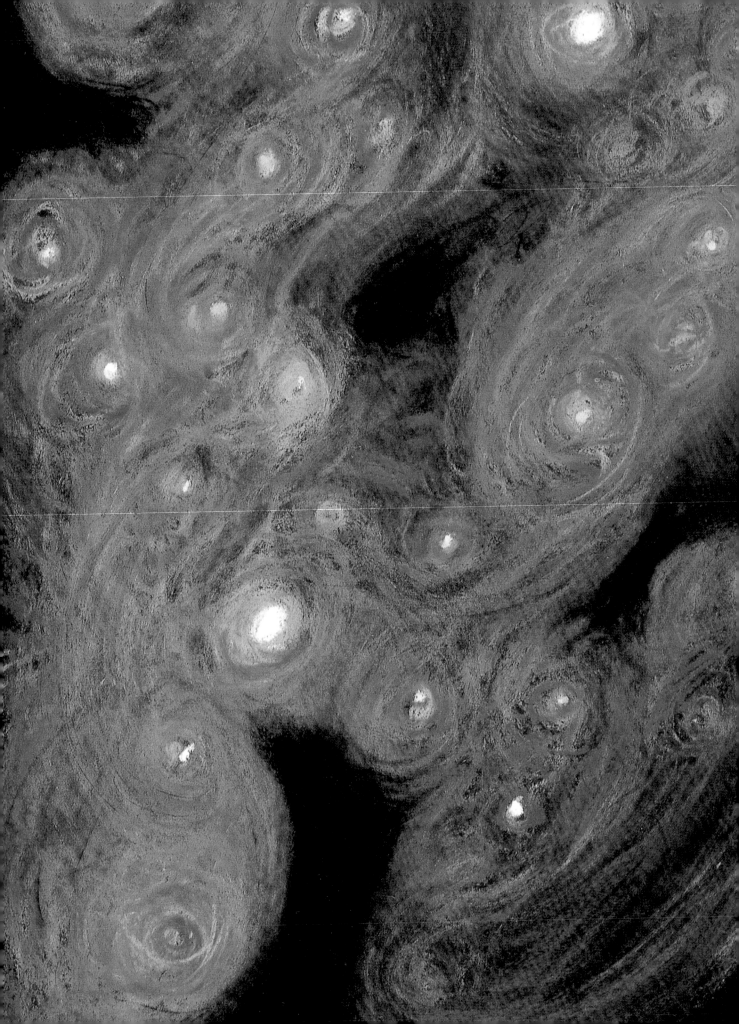

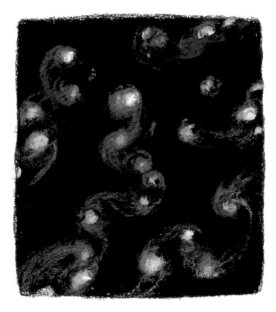

THE
GREAT
BEAR

LIBBY GLEESON & ARMIN GREDER

CANDLEWICK PRESS

Once there was a bear.

A circus bear.

A dancing circus bear.

All day she lay in a cage where the floor was cold, hard stone on her paws.

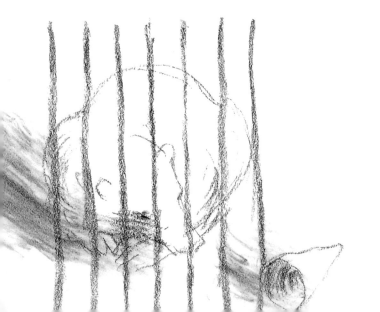

At night, by the light of flaming torches, she was led to the center of the square, where acrobats and tumblers, trapeze artists and clowns, performed for the crowd.

And she, too, performed.

To the music of trumpets, drums, and cymbals, she danced.
She lifted her feet and swayed to the sound, and some in the
crowd clapped and cheered. Others poked her with sticks
and threw stones at her ragged coat.

Day in and day out.

Year in and year out.

One night, high in the mountains, she was led
into the village square.

"It's the bear," called the crowd.
"It's the bear."
"Dance, bear, dance."

The bear stood very still.

"Dance, bear, dance."

She looked around.

"Dance, bear, dance."

Hear the music,
hear the music.
Trumpets blast,
drums roll.
Cymbals clash,
            clash,
                clash.

Sticks poke.
Sticks prod.
Chains yank.
Stones strike,
strike,
strike.

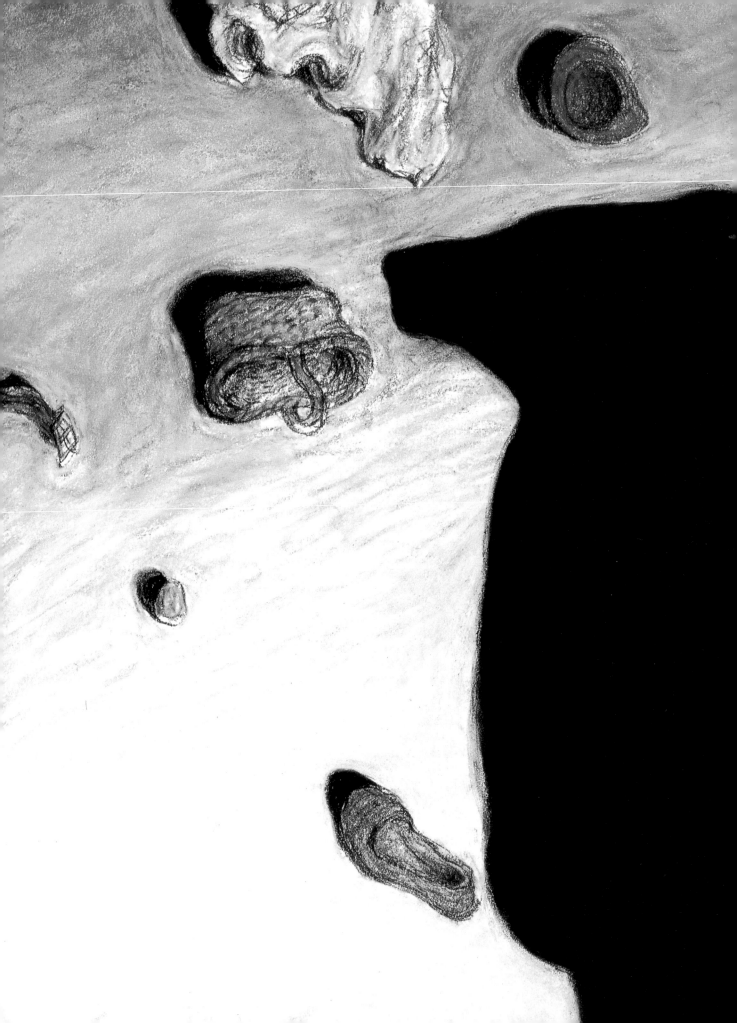

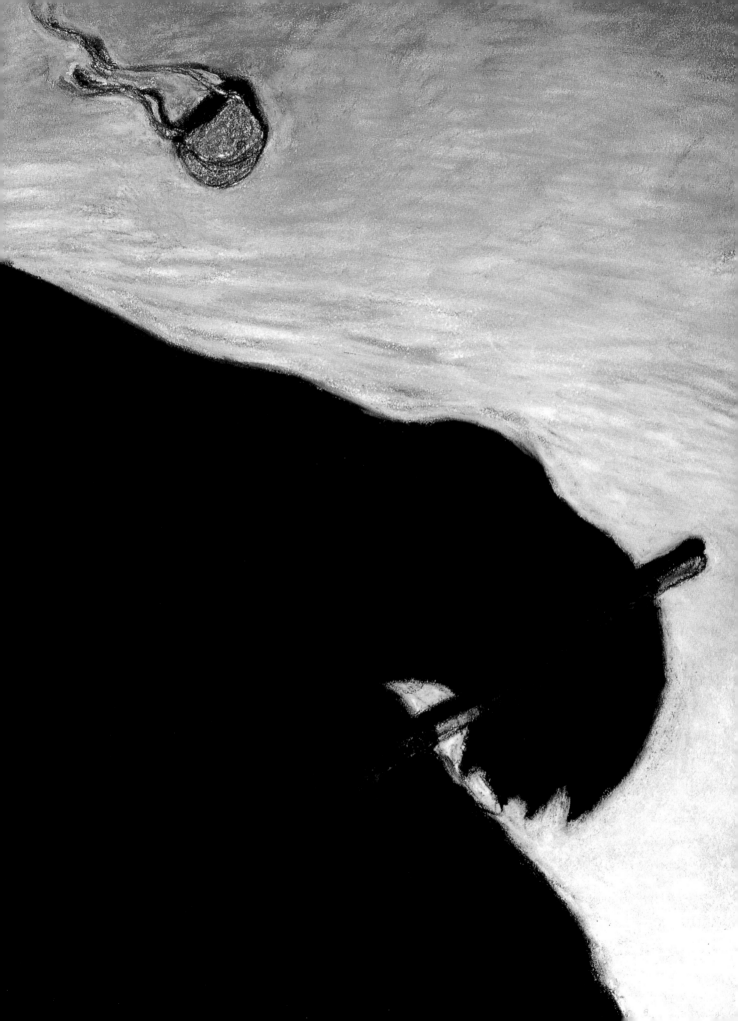

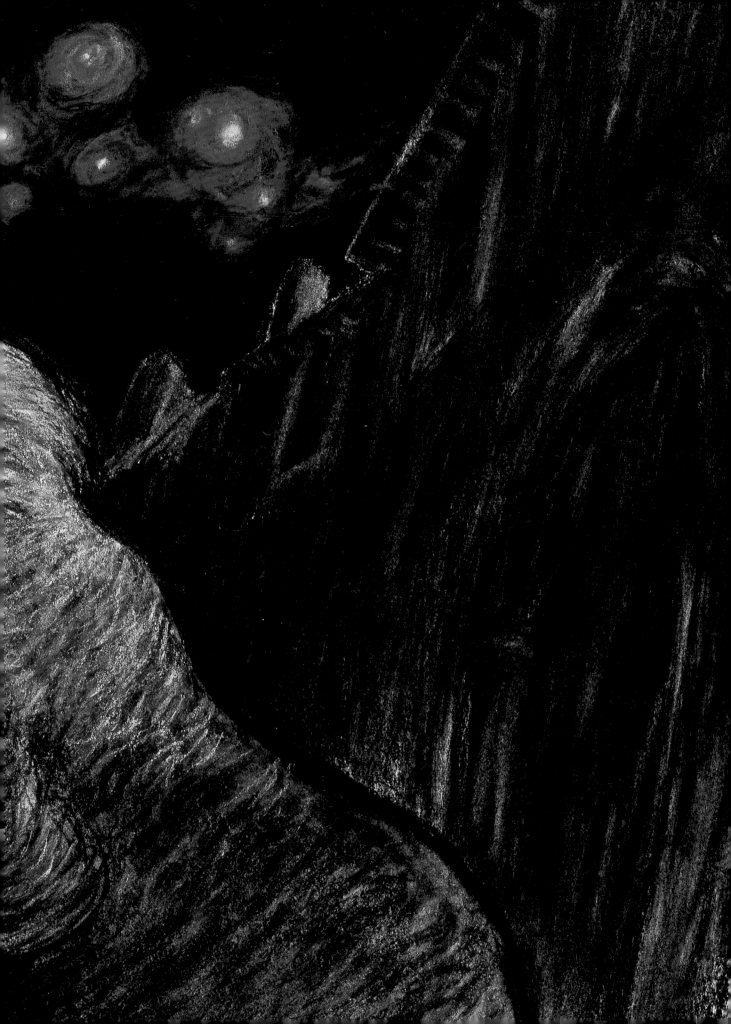

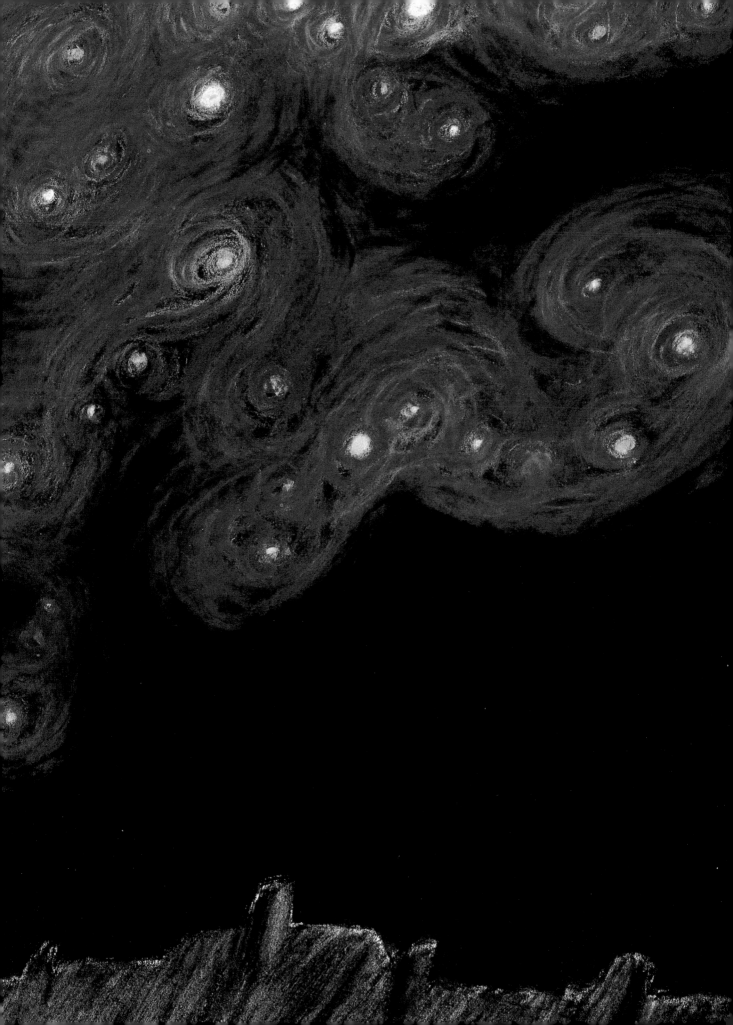

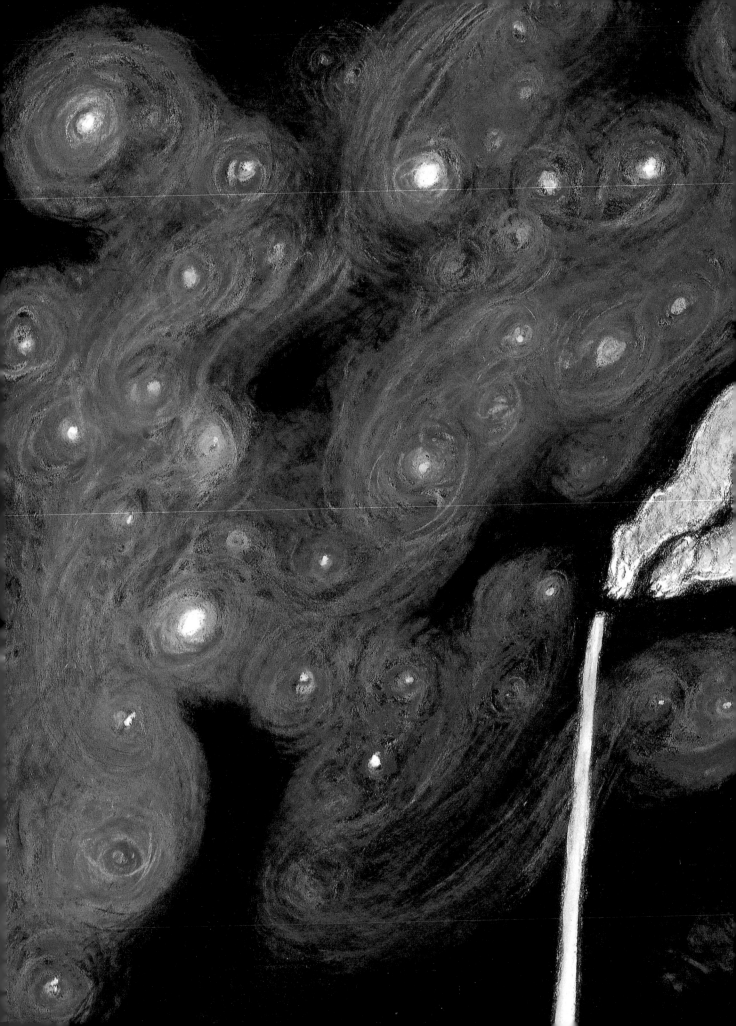

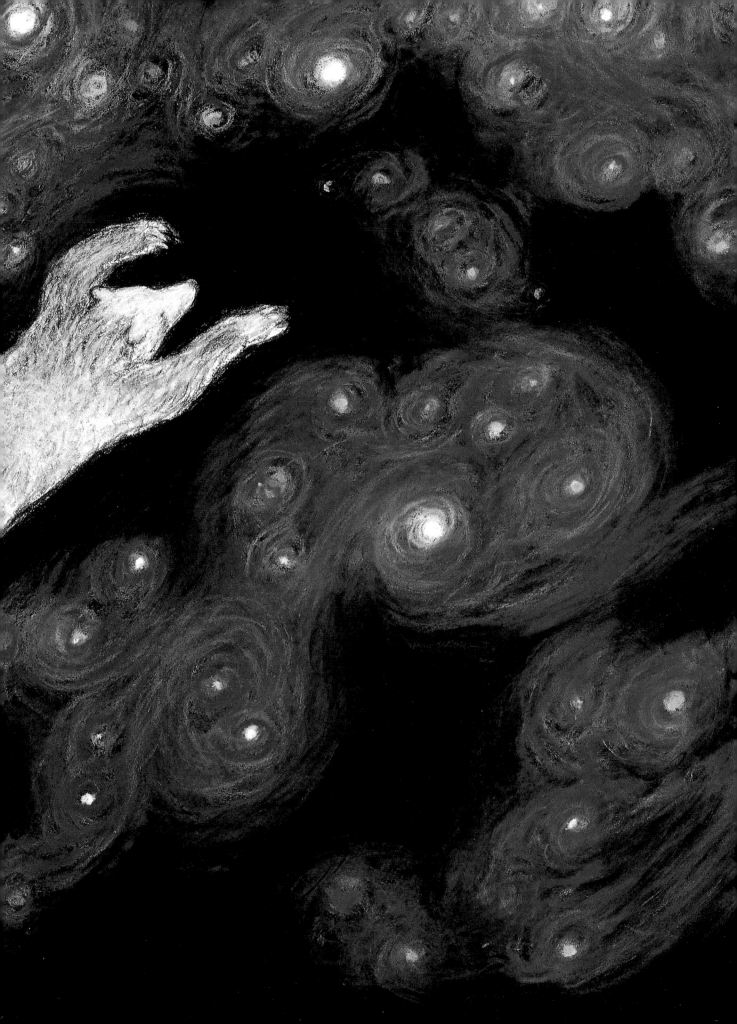

For Maurice Saxby
    L. G.

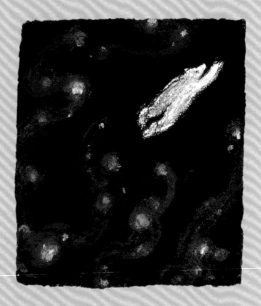

First U.S. edition 2011

This book was first published by
Scholastic Australia Pty Ltd., 1999

Library of Congress Cataloging-in-Publication Data

Gleeson, Libby.
The great bear / Libby Gleeson ;
[illustrations by Armin Greder]. — 1st U.S. ed.
p.   cm.
The Children's Book Council of Australia short-listed book
Bologna Ragazzi award winner, 2000
Summary: A bear imprisoned in a medieval circus
is forced to perform night after night before a
mocking crowd, but she finally can no longer stand
the torment and determines to set herself free.
ISBN 978-0-7636-5136-7
1. Bears—Juvenile fiction.
[1. Bears—Fiction. 2. Freedom—Fiction.]
I. Greder, Armin, ill. II. Title.
PZ10.3.G475Gr 2011
[E]—dc22   2010040288

17 16 15 14 13 12 11
SCP 10 9 8 7 6 5 4 3 2 1

Printed in Humen, Dongguan, China

This book was typeset in Bodoni Antiqua.
The illustrations were done in charcoal and pastels.

Candlewick Press
99 Dover Street
Somerville, Massachusetts 02144

visit us at www.candlewick.com

THE GREAT BEAR

Although I'm no expert in publishing, it is my understanding that it's quite unusual for an author and illustrator to collaborate intensively on a book from its inception. *The Great Bear* is one example of Libby Gleeson and Armin Greder's wonderful and award-winning partnership. Libby dreamed the story and shared it with Armin very early on in the writing process. One of the significant and bold decisions they made after much reflection was to leave the final half of the book devoid of written text. This creates the space for the reader to imagine what happened through the powerful visual images. There is a dramatic contrast between the bear in the two halves of the book. At the beginning she is depicted as oppressed, but midway through the story she takes control.

For me, another of this book's great strengths is that it has a number of different layers, stories within stories. On the surface, it is a poignant story set in medieval times. A dancing circus bear is so cruelly treated that she finally manages to flee her captors and escape into the heavens. Her magical release can be seen as the famous constellation, Ursa Major, in Northern Hemisphere skies. But the story is also an important metaphor about our right to live in freedom and with dignity. Sadly there are many examples around the world where this is not the case. *The Great Bear* is thus a timeless reminder that we all need to be valued, treated with respect, and allowed to be who we are.

Robyn Ewing
Professor of Teacher Education and the Arts
Faculty of Education and Social Work
University of Sydney, Australia

Libby Gleeson grew up in a number of country towns in Australia. She trained as a teacher, but gave it up to travel and to write. She lived in Europe and England for five years and has since returned to Australia, where she writes full-time. Libby has written more than thirty books for young readers, including picture books, middle-grade fiction, fiction for older readers, and nonfiction. Libby's work has received high acclaim both internationally and in Australia and has won many awards. Her books have been short-listed nine times for the Children's Book Council of Australia Awards, and Libby has won several times, with *Hannah Plus One* (Fiction for Young Readers Book of the Year), *An Ordinary Day* (Picture Book of the Year), and *Amy and Louis* (Early Childhood Book of the Year). Libby received the prestigious Lady Cutler Award for Services to Children's Literature in 1997.

Some of Libby's other books include the picture book *Cuddle Time*, illustrated by Julie Vivas, and the illustrated fiction title *Happy Birthday x 3*.

From Libby Gleeson:

I don't usually remember my dreams, but one morning I woke up with the night's dream firmly imprinted on my mind. It was the sequence of the events that now form the story. I didn't understand why I had dreamed this, but I was determined to remember the images. I told Armin Greder of the dream, and he urged me to write the story. He sent me small drawings of bears, and I began to write.

At first I simply relayed the events as I remembered them but then I developed a strong feeling that this was not simply a book about dancing bears; it was a story of inhumanity and the need to set oneself free.

The creation of this story was a genuine collaboration. Armin urged me to become more focused on myth and poetry in the writing. I urged him to create the sky as a character and to begin the work with the colorful landscape.

I have great confidence in his instincts as an illustrator, and when he asked me to drop the text in the second half of the book, I barely hesitated. The response of readers to the silence of the final pages of *The Great Bear* indicates that we made the right decision.